For Casey and Miles, in memory of Michael Wells Eisenhour, your
beloved father and my beloved husband. —L.A.

For my mom and pop. Thank you. ❤️🤗 —K.L.

The Family Business
Text copyright © 2022 by Lenore Appelhans
Illustrations copyright © 2022 by Ken Lamug
All rights reserved. Manufactured in Italy.

Library of Congress Control Number: 2021938239
ISBN 978-0-06-289886-9

The artist used pen and paper, digital ink, and good vibes
to create the illustrations on this book.
22 23 24 25 26 RTLO 10 9 8 7 6 5 4 3 2 1
❖
First Edition

# THE FAMILY BUSINESS

STORY BY Lenore Appelhans

PICTURES BY Ken Lamug

**HARPER**

*An Imprint of HarperCollinsPublishers*

Lucky felt like the luckiest raccoon in the world.

He had a big, boisterous family: Mama and Pop and three brothers, Hobart, Zed, and Ike.

The family worked hard to put tasty morsels on the table. They called it the *family business.*

Every day, Lucky asked, "When will I be able to join the family business, Pop?"
"Not until you're big enough."

So while his family went about their business, Lucky stayed home with their tiny TV.

His favorite show was *Everyone Loves Dancing!* This week's dance was the Jookery Jig.

"Breakfast time!" Mama called. Lucky danced his way up to a table stacked high with meatballs, marshmallows, and moldy melons.

"May I have a piece of moldy melon, please?" Lucky asked.

"Eat up," Mama said. "So you can get nice and big."

After breakfast, Lucky stood up tall for Pop. "Look, Son. You are finally big enough to join the family business."

HOME SWEET HOME

Lucky's brothers groaned. "But he'll mess everything up.
All Lucky does is dance!"
So Lucky decided he better not mess up . . .

First they went to Cordy's Cookies and Pickles, where Hobart dove into the dumpster.

Mama squealed in delight as he emerged with his paws full. "Such rancid and robust radishes," she said. "Hobart is my boy!"

Lucky loved the excitement of the family business, but Cordy's shouting hurt his ears.

At the fairgrounds, Zed cannonballed into a compost pile. When he surfaced with his spoils, Mama jumped for joy. "Such stringy and mushy corncobs!" she said. "Zed is my boy."

COMPOST ONLY

Lucky liked being part of the crew, but this business made his head pound.

The third stop was Farmer Ollie's Orchard, where Ike darted under the fence to load up his arms with fruit.

Mama took a big bite. "Such mealy and wormy apples!" she said. "Ike is my boy!"

Lucky was beginning to have second thoughts about the family business. It gave him a giant stomachache.

Back home, Lucky did not dance the Jookery Jig or a waltz or even a polka.

He stamped his foot and said, "Our family business isn't a business at all, and I don't want to do it."

"Lucky, you are part of our family and you will do as we do. Now go out and make us proud."

Lucky didn't want to get chased by anyone for taking their stuff, but he did want to please his pop. "Okay, I will try," he said, and left the house.

First Lucky returned to Cordy's with some coins he found.

No one made a fuss when he bought a sticky bun, and Cordy's "thank you" sounded pleasant to his ears.

But before he could bring it back to his family,
he got hungry and ate it.

Next Lucky made his way to the fairgrounds. He hoped his sweetest expression could score him some popcorn.
A kind lady gave him a whole bag. That didn't make his head pound at all.

But before he could even crunch a kernel, a bird flew off with it.

Finally Lucky tried Farmer Ollie's. Outside the window, he heard the sound of his favorite TV show.

While *Everyone Loves Dancing!* flashed on the giant TV, Lucky thought about how his family watched the *Varmint News* every evening. If Lucky borrowed this TV, they could watch it in style tonight!

Lucky waited patiently for Farmer Ollie's children to leave the room, but suddenly one of the children turned and screamed,

**"Look, the cutest raccoon ever!"**

Lucky didn't know whether to run away or play dead.

So instead . . .

he danced the Jookery Jig.

The children began recording
a video. Lucky danced his heart
out, imagining he was the star of
*Everyone Loves Dancing!*

Lucky had enjoyed performing for the children, and his stomach had not ached once.

But he did not enjoy Pop's disappointment when he came home. Lucky, it seemed, was in no way cut out for the family business.

After an awkward dinner, the family sat in front of the tiny TV to watch the *Varmint News*. The news announcer appeared.

"Tonight's feel-good story! Dancing raccoon steals a little girl's heart—her brother's—and ours, too!"

"Wow," said Lucky. "Maybe I didn't mess up after all."

Now whenever the family goes out, people recognize Lucky and ask him to dance his Jookery Jig. Most of the time, they give him treats, too.

"Such energetic and joyful dancing!" said Mama. "Lucky is my boy!"

"Now this," Pop said, "is what I call a family business!"